the Spelling Bee SCUFFLE

the Spelling Bee SCUFFLE

LINDSAY EYRE

ILLUSTRATED BY
SYDNEY HANSON

ARTHUR A. LEVINE BOOKS
AN IMPRINT OF SCHOLASTIC INC.

Library of Congress Cataloging-in-Publication Data

Names: Eyre, Lindsay, author. | Hanson, Sydney, illustrator.
Title: The spelling bee scuffle / Lindsay Eyre ; illustrated by Sydney
    Hanson.
Description: First edition. | New York, NY : Arthur A. Levine Books,
    an imprint of Scholastic Inc., 2016. | © 2016 | Series: [Sylvie Scruggs] |
    Summary: There is only one baseball field available for the children at
    Cherry Hill Elementary, and Jamie Redmond and the fifth graders
    insist that they have priority, so fourth grader Sylvie suggests that they
    let the school spelling bee decide—and then finds herself willing do
    anything, including cheating and agreeing to be the girlfriend of
    Daniel Fink, a boy who is made fun of by the other students because
    he has an artificial leg, to ensure that her grade wins.
Identifiers: LCCN 2015042705| ISBN 9780545620314 (hardcover : alk.
    paper)
Subjects: LCSH: Spelling bees—Juvenile fiction. | Competition
    (Psychology)—Juvenile fiction. | Cheating (Education)—
    Juvenile fiction. | People with disabilities—Juvenile fiction. |
    Bullying—Juvenile fiction. | Conduct of life—Juvenile fiction. |
    Friendship—Juvenile fiction. | CYAC: Spelling bees—Fiction. |
    Competition (Psychology)—Fiction. | Cheating—Fiction. | People
    with disabilities—Fiction. | Bullying—Fiction. | Conduct of life—
    Fiction. | Schools—Fiction.
Classification: LCC PZ7.1.E97 Sp 2016 | DDC 813.6—dc23 LC record
    available at http://lccn.loc.gov/2015042705

For Lucy, my sweet girl and
my kindest editor.

Chapter 1

It was a normal Tuesday in April, and I was at school, because in April I'm always in school. The bell rang for recess at ten forty-five, just like normal. I grabbed the bats; my friend, Georgie Diaz, grabbed two balls; and we ran out to the upper baseball field, just like normal.

But the field was not empty like normal. It was filled with fifth graders, including Jamie Redmond and her munions — two of the meanest girls at Cherry Hill Elementary. They had bats and balls and mitts. They had smirkety smirks on their faces.

"What are they doing?" Georgie said.

"Maybe they want to play baseball with us," said Josh Stetson, another one of my good friends. A clump of kids had gathered around us. There were tall ones and small ones. Girls and boys. Fourth graders like Georgie, Josh, Miranda, and me; third graders like my friend Alistair Robinson; and even some second graders. There were people who were great athletes, and people who weren't. We were all very different, but we had one thing in common: we loved baseball and this was our field.

"They don't look like they want to play with us," Alistair said.

"Um, can you go away?" Georgie politely called to the fifth graders. "We want to play baseball now."

The fifth graders looked at each other. They all rolled their eyes at the exact same time, like their eyeballs were tied together with invisible string. Then they laughed, especially the munions. "You can't play on *this* field," munion number one said.

"Why don't you go down to *your* field?" I said, but as I turned to look at the lower field where the fifth graders usually played baseball, I saw the answer to that question.

"Uh-oh," Miranda Tan, my best friend in the universe, whispered.

The fifth grade's field was down the hill at the very bottom of Cherry Hill's playground. Someone had surrounded it with bright orange tape, parked a tractor on the pitcher's mound, and dumped bags the size of pillows everywhere.

"They're tearing it up to make a fancy playground for the kindergartners," Jamie Redmond said, her voice full of disgust. "Principal Stoddard wants the little kids to run up and down the hill as much as possible so they are exhausted and ready for a nap after recess. My mom tried to stop it, but the principal said the kindergarteners were just as important as the fifth graders. Even though that's not true."

An invisible part of me understood the principal's point, because my twin brothers were kindergarteners and it was always better when they were sound asleep. But the visible part of me opened my mouth in disgust and outrage. "Then where are you guys going to play baseball?" I said.

Smirks spread over the fifth graders' faces like poison oak. "Right here," munion number one said.

I looked at my baseball friends. There were sixteen of us altogether. None of us smirked. "But we play here!" I said.

"Maybe we'll have to take turns," Miranda said. "We could play every other day."

"But what would we do on the days when we don't play baseball?" said a small girl on our team. Her name was Giselle, she was in third grade, and she sometimes put her clothes on inside out. She didn't have a lot of friends.

"There's nothing else to do!" cried another kid, whose name was Tiger. Tiger was in second grade and he wasn't very tigerish. Mean kids called him Tiger the Cry-ger.

"We are *not* taking turns," Jamie Redmond said. "We have to play baseball every day — tryouts for the town league begin in two weeks."

"Some of us are trying out too!" I said.

"But we're the ones who matter," munion number one said.

"Sylvie," Alistair said, sounding worried. "Are they going to take the field from us?" Before we played hockey together, Alistair had no one to hang out with at recess. Now he had baseball, and he had friends. He was probably afraid that if we lost the field, all of that would go away.

I looked around for help from someone — anyone — but everyone on our side just stood there with their mitts hanging down. The fifth graders were playing catch with their balls and swinging their bats. They weren't worried a bit.

"I'm sorry," Jamie Redmond said, because she's never nice, but sometimes she's almost nice. "This stinks for you guys."

"But *we're* the fifth graders," munion number one said. "So *we* get the field."

"No way!" Georgie shouted. "It doesn't matter what grade you're in!"

"You'll get the field when *you're* in fifth grade," munion number two called. The other fifth graders nodded. Giselle and Tiger looked as if their hearts would break.

"You should make a bet." The voice came from a group of trees near the outfield. We turned to see a huge kid I'd never noticed before, standing in the shadows by himself. "The winner of the bet gets the field," he continued. "That would be more fair."

"Shut up, Robot Boy," munion number one said.

"Yeah," said munion number two. "I bet you can't even play baseball with a robot leg."

Robot leg? I looked at the boy's legs but saw only pants.

"A bet's not a bad idea," Jamie Redmond said. "It would be more fair."

Georgie looked interested. "What sort of bet?"

"We could have a baseball game," Jamie Redmond said. "You guys versus us."

"No," I said quickly. The kids who played baseball with us were all great, except they weren't all great at baseball. We would lose a baseball game for sure.

"How about a race?" said munion number one, one of the fastest girls in the school.

"I don't think a race is a good idea," Miranda said.

"We could have a throwing competition," said one of the fifth grade's best throwers.

"No," Alistair said. "Your arms are longer."

"Or a hitting competition," said the fifth grade's best batter.

Georgie shook his head. "Bad idea, dude."

"Or a catching competition," said a great fifth grade catcher.

"No," Josh said, because he usually played catcher.

The fifth graders were bigger and stronger, and even if I was a great thrower thanks to all my pitching, and Georgie was an awesome hitter, it was too risky. Jamie *might* throw faster than me by accident. One of the stupid munions *might* get superpowers and hit the ball farther than Georgie.

"I don't think a bet is a very good idea," Josh said. "We should think of another way to figure this out."

The shouting began once again. I bit my lip, searching for an idea. There had to be something we could bet on that we were guaranteed to win.

Miranda put her arm around Alistair to comfort

him. She was always such a good friend to everyone, always trying to make people feel better. She was good at other things too, even if they weren't sports. Things like math and science and spelling.

I gasped. Miranda! Spelling! That was it! The class spelling bees were today, and Miranda would win for sure. She almost won the school spelling bee last year when she'd only been in third grade, and third graders never almost win spelling bees.

"I know!" I shouted, and everyone turned to me, because I am great at shouting. "The school spelling bee is next Monday. Whoever wins the bee will win the field!"

"The spelling bee?" Georgie said. He looked at Miranda.

"You mean, if a fifth grader wins the bee, the fifth grade gets the field?" munion number two said, smirking a smirkety smirk.

"Sylvie," Miranda said in a warning sort of voice.

"For the rest of the year?" Jamie Redmond said.

"Yes," I told Jamie. "And if a fourth grader wins the bee, we get the field for the rest of the year."

There were grumblings and whisperings behind me as our side talked about my idea — they were worried it wouldn't work and we would lose the field forever. I whispered to them that we had Miranda, the best speller in the universe, and they quieted down a little. The fifth graders were smiling and pointing at munion number two for some reason. That big, quiet boy was still standing in the trees, watching.

"What about this week?" munion number two said. "Who gets the field this week?"

"Nobody," I said, because I didn't want any of those munions playing on our field ever. "No one can play on the field until after the bee."

"What?" the kids on our side cried. "We have to play! What else will we do?"

Jamie Redmond and her fifth grade buddies

laughed at this. Like we were a bunch of baby losers who had no friends.

"So is it a deal?" I said loudly, my arms crossed, my face triumphant like an elephant. If they agreed, we would win the field for sure.

"It's a deal," Jamie said, and we shook on it.

Chapter 2

"Attention!" Ms. Bloomen said as soon as we were back in our seats after recess. "It's time for our class spelling bee!"

Some of the class cheered, but many of us did not. This was not because we didn't like spelling bees — spelling bees are always great, because if they last long enough, we don't have to do math. We didn't cheer because of the bet. Whoever won the class bee would go to the school spelling bee, and the future of baseball rested upon their spelling shoulders. No one wanted to have those shoulders.

I was one of the cheerers, because I wasn't worried. Miranda would win the spelling bee; the fifth graders would have to play hopscotch at recess, which would be funny; and everything would be just fine. Forever.

Miranda's eyes were on the clock, while her teeth were on her fingernails. "It's okay," I whispered to her. "You'll be great. You're practically the spelling champion of the universe!"

She gulped so loudly it sounded like she'd swallowed a baseball.

"Everyone line up!" Ms. Bloomen said. "That's right, over there. Near the windows. No jostling. Everyone be respectful!"

Nobody was respectful and everyone jostled, because no one wanted to go first. Most of the time our class was not very unified, but in this, we were awesomely one.

Ms. Bloomen began anyway. She started with really easy words like *across*, *again*, and *cellar*.

"A-C-R-O-S," Lucy Smith said.

"A-G-A-E-N," Seamus Holland answered.

"C-E-L-L-A-R-R," Marcie Xu said, taking an extra long time on the last letter, like a pirate.

"Three *r*'s, Marcie?" Ms. Bloomen said.

"Aren't there?" Marcie said, even though she is one of the smartest girls in the room.

The spelling bee went on. People were dropping like flies that didn't know how to spell.

"E-M-M-B-B-A-R-R-A-S-S."

"L-E-E-G."

"A-R-C-H-E-R-I-E."

Within minutes, only four people were left: me, Miranda, Georgie, and Josh. Miranda and Josh both looked as if they were going to throw up the

alphabet. *Come on, Miranda!* I thought at her. *You can do this! Spelling is easy for you!*

"I-N-T-E-R-N-A-T-I-O-N-A-L," Miranda spelled correctly.

"P-O-S-S-E-S-S," Josh spelled correctly.

"C-A-M-M-I-T-M-E-N-T," Georgie spelled incorrectly, possibly on purpose.

"P-A-S-T-T-I-M-E," I spelled incorrectly, not on purpose, because pastime is a word that should have two *t*'s even if it doesn't.

Only Miranda and Josh were left, which was great because Josh would get out any second.

"C-L-I-M-A-C-T-I-C," Miranda spelled.

"F-L-A-U-N-T," Josh spelled.

"W-I-D-G-E-T," spelled Miranda.

"R-I-T-Z-I-N-E-S-S," spelled Josh.

The words went on and on. "Correct!" Ms. Bloomen said again and again. I tapped my toe. I looked at my wrist as if I had a watch. Math time was over now — Josh needed to get out!

"*Trepidatious*," Ms. Bloomen said to Miranda.

My heart pinged. The clock ticked. That was a tough word, but Miranda could do it. She could spell anything.

"T-R-E-P-I-D-A-C-I-O-U-S," she said.

Ms. Bloomen shook her head. "That's incorrect."

My mouth dropped like a ball falling out of a window. She'd spelled it wrong.

"Now, Josh," Ms. Bloomen said. "If you get this word wrong, the rounds will continue and Miranda will get another chance. If you get this word right, you will be our classroom champion."

I looked at Josh with big eyes and pinched lips. It was my warning face that meant, "Spell this word wrong so that Miranda can win!" Josh looked right at me and nodded.

"Crescendo," Ms. Bloomen said, and I sighed in relief. That was a really hard word. Josh would never get it right.

"C-R-E-S-C-E-N-D-O," Josh said.

"Correct!" Ms. Bloomen cried. "Congratulations, Josh! Wonderful work. Josh is our class spelling champion! He will represent our class in the Cherry Hill spelling bee next Monday. Everyone give Josh a hand."

Ms. Bloomen didn't need to say this, because the class was already clapping their hands and stomping their feet. They were cheering because Josh is such a nice person, and it's nice when nice people win things. They were also cheering because they were glad it wasn't them.

I was not clapping, because even if I'd wanted to clap, I was too shocked to make my hands hit each other. Josh looked as stunned as I was. His mouth was open, his eyes were as round as eyeballs, and his eyebrows were as high as they could go.

Josh will never win the school spelling bee, I thought, *and we made that stupid bet, which was my idea in the first place.*

Josh put his head down on his desk.

"*Oh no,*" I whispered.

Chapter 3

My friends and I walked home together after school like normal, because even when bad stuff happens, you still have to walk home from school. Usually when we walk home, Miranda and I talk a lot while Georgie says some rude things and some not-so-rude things and Josh smiles. Alistair likes to add things to the conversation that he thinks are interesting.

Today, Miranda and I said nothing, Georgie looked too tired to be rude, and Josh did not smile.

"What's the matter with you guys?" Alistair said, because there was no conversation for him to add to.

"Josh won the class spelling bee," Miranda said slumpily. "Now he's nervous about being in the school bee."

"But I thought *you* were going to win!" Alistair said. "Sylvie promised! She said you were the best speller ever."

"I didn't study much this year," Miranda said. "I've been focused on the science fair."

"And I meant to lose," Josh said, shaking his head. "I didn't think crescendo had an *s*."

"It's okay, dude," Georgie said. "I thought it had an *s-h*."

"What's an *s-h*?" Alistair said. "Is that Latin?"

"How do you study for a spelling bee anyway?" Georgie said to Miranda. "Do you memorize the dictionary?"

"Alexa has," Josh said, speaking about munion number two as if she had a real name. He was looking as slumpy as I'd ever seen him. His skin was pale, almost green. "I heard Jamie talking about it in the hall after school. Alexa won the school spelling bee last year, and she won their class bee today. I'm going to be competing against her."

Georgie kicked at an invisible munion. "I didn't know she won the bee last year. Did you guys remember that?"

We shook our heads because we'd all forgotten.

Georgie went slumpy. "A spelling bee bet was a bad idea."

"I'm not good at memorizing dictionaries," Josh said. "Just multiplication tables."

"But you can't multiply spelling words," Alistair said. "This is a disaster!"

"Yeah," Josh said. "It is."

Everyone sighed but me. I crossed my arms and frowned my lips. Something was very wrong here. My friends were depressed and slumpy. Any second now they would shout, "The spelling bee was your idea! This is all your fault, Sylvie Scruggs!" I needed to do something fast.

"You've always been a good speller," I said to Josh.

Like magic, he stood up a little straighter.

"You're not like Georgie," I told him. "Ms. Bloomen doesn't make you redo your papers because you spelled so many things wrong."

"That's true," Georgie said, because he was excellent at math and didn't care about spelling.

Josh looked even less slumpy now, though he still looked a little sick.

"You've always been great at reading and writing," Miranda added.

"He has?" Alistair said with great doubtfulness.

I looked at Josh as if I knew a secret about him that no one else knew. "I think you'll win," I told him.

"Really?" he said.

"Of course!" Miranda cried. "You have plenty of time to study. It's Tuesday and the school bee isn't until Monday — that gives you six days."

"Seven if you count Monday," Georgie said.

"Five if you don't," Alistair said, because he wanted to say something important, even if it was wrong.

Josh almost looked like a happy person now. "I guess I could try," he said.

"Totally," Georgie said.

"You'll be awesome!" Miranda said.

"You *have* to be awesome," Alistair said.

"We'll help you," I said, trying not to smile too much, so my friends wouldn't know that I'd changed their minds without their permission.

★　★　★

When I walked into the kitchen later that afternoon, I found my brothers in the depths of despair. This was not entirely a surprise, because Cale is always in the depths of despair, while Tate is usually in the depths of trouble, but today, they looked like two Cales and no Tates. Both of them were flopped across the kitchen table like limp pieces of asparagus.

"What's the matter?" I demanded as I sat down with them.

"Lizards," Tate croaked.

"Eighteen lizards!" Cale moaned.

"You found eighteen lizards?" I asked. This would normally make my brothers really happy.

"Their kindergarten class is having a vote about which class pet to get," my mom explained. She was at the table too, feeding my baby sister, Ginny, something that looked like smashed asparagus. "They can choose between a rabbit and a lizard."

"Oh," I said, because everything made sense now. Thanks to a book about superhero rabbits with magic powers and vegetable weapons, Cale and Tate had recently decided to become magic bunnies. Not the kind of magic bunny that can jump out of a hat, but the kind of magic bunny that shoots lasers from its paws, strikes down enemies with one smack of its mighty powder-puff tail, and uses its teeth as boomerangs to retrieve stolen objects.

"There are eighteen other kids in our class," Cale said. "And they want a lizard."

Tate stabbed the table with an invisible carrot he held in his fist. "Thanks to Mary Fink and her robot brother."

"Robot brother?" I said. Hadn't the munions called that sad-looking boy a robot?

Cale put his forehead on the table. "Mary Fink is new and cool, and everyone wants a lizard just like her."

My brothers looked as slumpy as my friends had looked just minutes ago! I was fed up with slumpy people. One hundred percent fed up. "Stop it!" I said. "You can't take this lying down like lizards! You have to fight for your bunny!"

Tate looked at Cale. Cale looked at Tate. They both looked as if they wanted to fight for their bunny, but they didn't know how.

"She doesn't mean actually fighting, boys," my mom explained as she wiped smashed asparagus off Ginny's earlobe. "She means fighting like in a campaign." She took Ginny out of the kitchen to change her diaper.

"What's a can pane?" Cale said.

"A campaign is where you do things to make people pick what you want them to pick," I explained. I knew a lot about campaigns because my dad had told me stories about when he ran for student representative of his elementary school, and he almost won. Back in third grade, I ran for Cherry Hill student representative, and I also almost won.

"We're not picking anything," Cale said.

"Except for when Cale picks his nose," Tate said. "But that was yesterday."

"First, you'll need to make posters," I told them. "Positive pep talk posters that convince people that rabbits are the best. Second, you'll need a mascot — a really clever symbol that reminds people how awesome rabbits are."

"Wow!" Cale cried, jumping to his feet. "Those are great ideas! We'll make posters that say, *Lizards are bums*!"

"Yeah!" Tate shouted. "And a bloody lizard can be our mascot!"

"No," I said, because that was not positive pep talk. "Your mascot should be an awesome magic bunny, and your posters should have pictures of muscley rabbits. They should say stuff like *Rabbits Rock* and *Rabbits to the Rescue* and *Rabbits Can Perform Feats of Amazing Wonder!*"

"Rabbits do have amazing feet," Cale said, and without even saying, "Thank you for your brilliant idea, great sister," my brothers jumped up from the table and ran to their room to start their campaign.

I smiled as I watched them go. Josh would study and do a fantastic job and win the spelling bee. My brothers would work hard on their campaign, and the kindergarten would get a rabbit for a class pet. Everything would work out just fine. No problem.

Chapter 4

On Wednesday morning, I walked across the street and picked up Miranda. We went to Georgie's house next, then up the street to where we usually met Alistair and Josh. I was very excited to see Josh. I'd planned out five positive pep talk things to say to him about spelling, just like I'd used on my brothers the day before. I was sure they would give him the extra happiness he needed to become a brilliant speller.

But Alistair was waiting for us alone.

"Where's Josh?" I said.

"Sick," Alistair said. "Stomach flu, which is really gross, because it means he's been throwing up and throwing up and throwing up, and it's probably gotten all over his house and his bed and in his hair, because he probably wiped it on his face when he was finished. Then he probably threw up again."

"Dude!" Georgie said, which in Georgie-talk meant, "That is so disgusting! Shut up!"

"I know," Alistair said, because he doesn't speak Georgie-talk. "Stomach flu is the worst. I got it last year on Thanksgiving, but I didn't know I had it until I'd eaten turkey and some pumpkin pie, and when I threw up —"

"Poor Josh!" Miranda said loudly. "I hope it's not one of those weeklong flus!"

"Weeklong flus?" Alistair said, forgetting about throwing up turkey. "It can't last a week. He'll miss the bee!"

Georgie shrugged. "It's probably a three-day flu. Calm down, dude."

"But if Josh misses the bee, the fifth graders will win!" Alistair turned to me. "This is your fault, Sylvie. We shouldn't have made the bet. Now Josh won't be able to spell, and we'll lose the baseball field!"

Alistair had never yelled at me before. He wasn't a yelling sort of person, but at this moment, he looked as if he might punch me in the elbow.

I squeezed my brains for something to say that would calm Alistair down. Something my mom might say to my brothers when they were upset. "Even if we lose the bet *and* the baseball field, the world won't explode," I said. "A volcano won't erupt. A dinosaur won't eat the baseball field."

My friends stared at me for a moment, probably picturing a dinosaur eating the baseball field.

"If we can't play baseball, recess will be ruined!" Alistair said. He ran off then as if he wanted to get far, far away from me.

Miranda patted me on the backpack. "Don't worry. Even if Josh loses, another fourth grader might win. We haven't lost yet."

"I'm not worried," I said, stepping away from her pats. "We aren't going to lose, but even if we did, everything will be fine. Perfectly, totally fine!"

When the bell rang for recess, I looked at the baseball equipment sitting on the shelves and sighed. Georgie and Miranda sighed too. "We'll find something awesome to do today," I said. "Something even more fun than baseball."

Georgie raised his eyebrows at me, because his eyebrows knew the truth. Nothing was more fun than baseball.

"It's just for one week!" I said. Then I stormed out into the hallway where I ran straight into

Giselle. I was just helping her up when I saw the rest of the kids we played baseball with. Twelve kids plus Alistair, standing in the hall, waiting for me.

"Whoa," Georgie said as he and Miranda left our classroom. "What are you guys doing here?"

"We don't have anything to do at recess," Giselle announced.

"The baseball field is the only place we can go," said a big kid named Ezekiel.

The rest nodded and began telling stories about how they had no friends or they were allergic to the monkey bars or the girls on the merry-go-round threw pebbles at them whenever they tried to get on.

Miranda, of course, tried to comfort everyone by patting them on the elbows and saying things weren't so bad. It was just for a week.

"Unless Josh loses the spelling bee," Georgie said unhelpfully, which made Giselle cry.

"What are we going to do, Sylvie?" everyone seemed to say at once.

I looked at them, looking at me, acting as if it were my job to make sure they had fun at recess. "It's not fair!" I wanted to shout. "Not everything is my fault! Can't you all think for yourselves?"

I did not shout this. That would only make the rest of them cry.

"I'm sure there is something you can do at recess," I said, and when they opened their mouths to tell me there wasn't, I flapped my hands so they wouldn't speak. "You will be *fine*," I said with invisible italic letters. Georgie and Miranda nodded their agreement, which gave me a fantastic idea. "Georgie, Miranda, and I will help you find an activity on the playground today. Then you will see that even if Josh loses the spelling bee — which he will not, because he is awesome — you will not die. A sea monster will not leap out of the nearest swimming pool to swallow you whole."

"There are sea monsters in swimming pools?" Tiger squeaked.

"Georgie, you take Tiger and Natalie and those other kids down to the soccer field," I told him, pointing to the kids who were pretty good at baseball and might like soccer. "Miranda, you take Ezekiel and Youmee and those other kids over to the swings and the monkey bars," I said, pointing to the kids who had long arms and seemed like they might enjoy playing circus. "I'll take Giselle and Alistair over to the playground."

"The playground!" Alistair said. "No way, Sylvie! You don't understand. You don't know what it's like on the playground!"

"Yes, I do," I said, taking Giselle by the hand. "I used to play on the playground before I played baseball. Back when I was in kindergarten. It wasn't that bad!" I took Alistair's elbow, and together we walked across the blacktop to the section where kids played games like tag and capture the mountain. It was a pretty new playground with ramps and wobbly bridges and ladders and forts. I'd always thought it might be fun if I didn't have more important things to do like baseball.

"This is Giselle," I said to a girl who was standing in the middle of a wobbly bridge, counting to ten. Giselle began tugging on my shirt, but I ignored her. "Can she play hide-and-go-seek with you guys?"

"We're not playing hide-and-go-seek," the girl said, covering her eyes. "Four, five!"

"Then what are you playing?" I said loudly so she would pause her rude counting.

"Six, seven — we're playing something else," she said.

"Can Giselle play?" I said, beginning to get annoyed with this girl, who sounded a lot like munion number one and munion number two.

The girl spread her fingers apart so I could see one of her eyes. "No," she said. "That would be too many people. Whenever Giselle wants to play, it is always too many people. Eight, nine, ten! Here I come!" and she darted off like a big jerk who purposely hurts other people's feelings because she is a big jerk.

"Hopscotch," I said before Giselle's almost tearful face turned into an all-the-way tearful face. "Kids who play hopscotch aren't mean." I grabbed Giselle's hand and Alistair's elbow and pulled them over to the row of hopscotch squares that lined the edge of the blacktop. There were six hopscotch boards on the playground and all of them were full. I scanned each one, looking for the group of kids that was the smallest and the nicest. One group didn't wear any smirks and was made up of kids of all ages and sizes, boys and girls.

"But we don't know how to play hopscotch," Alistair said as I led them over to this group.

"I'll show you," I said. I'd never played hopscotch before, but I knew you threw a hopscotch puck-thingy and counted to ten and then hopped on one leg until you got to the other side of the squares. "Can we play too?" I asked a very nice-looking boy whose name was probably Timothy.

"Sure," he said with a big smile. I grinned at Giselle and Alistair to show them that some people on playgrounds can be nice. Timothy handed me the hopscotch puck-thingy and told me to take a turn.

I stood at one end of the squares, the end with the number one on it, took a deep breath, and threw the puck-thingy gently across the squares. "I did it!" I cried, because the puck-thingy did not touch any lines and it made it to the other side, close to the ten. Then I jumped into box number one and began hopping up and down on one leg, because that's what people did when they hopscotched. I tried turning around in a circle while I was hopping, but this made me dizzy, which made me fall over.

"Okay, you lose," said Timothy, still smiling.

"I didn't lose," I said.

"You did," said another girl who also probably had a *T* name, like Theresa or Tasmania. "You missed square one."

"I hopped up and down in square one," I said, demonstrating what I'd done.

"You have to throw the shooter into square one first," said another boy.

"The shooter?" I said, because no one said anything about shooting, which I was against.

"Here, I'll show you," said a girl whose name was probably Brenda. She picked up the puck-thingy and walked over to square one. "Say I'm on number seven," she said. "I throw the shooter into square seven." She threw the shooter into the square with a seven on it and turned around so she was standing on one leg and facing me. Then she hopped backward inside the squares from one to six. Like a flamingo, she leaned over on one leg, picked up the shooter, flipped around and jumped backward all the way to square one. "See!" she said. "It's easy!"

"You don't have to jump backward," said the *T*-name boy.

"That's just a harder way to do it," said Theresa or Tasmania.

"I've been hopscotching since I was three," Brenda explained, as if this made hopping backward like a flamingo any less annoying. "You've never played before, right? That's so weird — how old are you?"

I stood up tall and looked wisely at the hop-scotchers. "It doesn't matter if I've never played hopscotch before because it is not a real sport. Thank you for your time." Then I gathered Alistair and Giselle by the elbows and dragged them away again.

"Where are we going now?" Alistair asked.

I stopped for a moment and looked around. Kids were everywhere, controlling the playground equipment, being bossy on the swings, not letting people on the soccer field — telling everyone what to do. There really was nowhere for us to go.

"The baseball field," I finally said, because it was the only place left.

Chapter 5

Georgie and his group met us on our way down the hill. "Soccer!" he said with great disgust. "What a stupid sport. That ball is huge! All you can do is kick it!"

Ezekiel leaned close to me and whispered loud enough for everyone to hear, "The soccer ball hit him in the face."

"Wow!" Alistair said. "Right in the face? Does that mean they let you play?"

"No," Georgie said in a way that told everyone they'd better not ask how he got hit in the face with the ball when he wasn't even playing. "They said only the 'soccer kids' could play."

Miranda's group appeared then. They looked as if they'd all been hit in the face by a soccer ball. Miranda's arms were crossed with madness. "I can't believe how rude people are!" she said. "They said we didn't belong on that part of the playground! They wouldn't even share the monkey bars!"

"Shhhh!" I said, because that meant there was truly nothing for us to do.

"Hey," Georgie said, pointing to the baseball field. "Is that those fifth graders? Are they playing ball?"

We gasped a group gasp, then took off for the field as fast as angry baseballers could go.

"You aren't supposed to be here!" I shouted at Jamie Redmond. She sat on the pitcher's mound with the rest of the fifth graders surrounding her. They weren't playing baseball, but they had the necessary equipment. They looked ready to play.

"We're not playing baseball," munion number two announced as she tossed a ball up in the air.

"Yeah," said munion number one. "We're having a mock spelling bee."

I narrowed my eyes at this, because spelling bees were not about mocking people. Unless you were a munion, of course. Then you mocked everything.

"You should probably do a mock spelling bee with Josh," Jamie Redmond said in her I-know-everything-you-don't-know way. "It will help him so he's not nervous."

"Josh won't get nervous," I said. "And we don't mock people for fun. Not even in spelling bees."

The fifth graders looked at each other and burst out laughing, ha ha ha. "A *mock* spelling bee works

44

like this," munion number one said. She turned to munion number two. "Spell *radioactive isotope*," she said.

Munion number two took a deep breath. "R-A-D-I-O-A-C-T-I-V-E *space* I-S-O-T-O-P-E."

"That's two words," Miranda said. "You don't get two words at once in spelling bees."

"This is an extra-tough mock bee," munion number one said.

"*So*," I said, crossing my arms so I looked extra-tough. "Josh could totally spell radioactive isomotrope."

"*Isotope*," Miranda whispered.

"Either one," I whispered back.

The fifth graders didn't argue with me like I expected. They just smirked, then, following munion number one's orders, lined up one by one with munion number two at the head of the line. As they walked by her, they said a really hard word that she spelled lightning fast.

"This is boring," I said loudly. Then I pointed in the direction of the school so my team would follow me up the hill, away from those show-offs.

Miranda motioned to the dejecticated faces of our friends. "This is awful," she whispered.

"Josh is going to beat the pants off those jerks," Georgie said.

"We should do a mock spelling bee too," Alistair said. "Tomorrow at recess. We'll show them how good Josh is at spelling, right, Sylvie?"

I considered this. It wasn't a bad idea, as long as Josh had been studying. If he had, it would shut up those stupid munions and make munion number two afraid of losing. Plus, it would help our baseball friends know that they should listen to me more often because most of my ideas are good.

"We'll have a real *pretend* spelling bee at recess tomorrow so you guys can see how great a speller Josh is," I announced to our side. "Everyone come prepared with really tough words to give him."

"That's a great idea!" Ezekiel said.

"I can't wait for tomorrow!" Tiger shouted.

The bell rang. I took Giselle's hand so if the mean hide-and-seek girl saw us, she would know that some people liked to play with Giselle. I didn't notice the sad-looking boy until we were nearly off the field. He was standing in the trees again, watching, and when he caught me looking at him, he nodded as if he'd just heard everything I said and knew what I meant by it.

"Ms. Bloomen?" a voice said over the intercom later that afternoon, during the middle of silent sustained reading.

Ms. Bloomen's head jerked up from off her desk. "What's the matter?" she cried. "Be quiet!"

"Ms. Bloomen?" the voice said again, and I recognized it now. It was the voice of my good friend, Mr. Root, the assistant principal. "I need Sylvie Scruggs down at the office right now, please."

"Sylvie?" Ms. Bloomen said. She pushed at her

messed-up hair with her hand. She looked at me as if I'd been the one to mess it up.

"Sylvie didn't do anything wrong," Mr. Root said. "It's her brothers. They're missing."

One second later, I was in the main office. "Have you checked the toilets?" I asked Mr. Root. "When they were little, they used to climb into the toilets to play. Sometimes they'd get stuck."

"I believe the bathrooms have been checked," Mr. Root said. He was a shortish man with a jolly smile. His head reminded me of my baby sister's head, because they were both mostly bald. "Your mother is on her way, but do you have any other ideas?"

I thought as hard as I could imagine thinking. "They want to be magic bunnies," I told him. "Are there any thickets nearby?"

A wrinkle popped up on his forehead. "No, not on school property."

"What about briar patches?"

Two wrinkles appeared. "All plants with thorns have been banished from the playground, but you've given me an idea. Will you stay here in the office, in case your mother arrives? I'll be right back. Don't touch anything!"

Suddenly, I was alone, and then, suddenly, I wasn't, because the door opened again. It was that big kid always standing in the trees by the field! He was very unusual-looking, with messy dark hair and large, squinty eyes. His nose looked like an enormous shell tilting downward. He reminded me of a high school person, only sleepier.

He walked toward the secretary's desk where I stood, and I noticed something else: He walked funny. One foot fell down faster than the other, as if it wasn't sure what it was supposed to do. Was that his robot leg?

"What are you doing here?" I said.

"I'm looking for Mr. Root." The boy's voice was quiet and grumbly.

I did not want to stand too close to him, so I walked around the secretary's desk and sat down in her chair. "He's not here," I said.

Without my permission, the boy sat down in a chair against the wall.

"He might not get back for a long time," I said.

"I'll wait," he said.

"Waiting will be boring," I warned.

"S'okay," he said.

"You could be here forever."

"S'all right," he said.

I puffed out my lips. I sighed a big sigh. I tried to look busy and annoyed, but he did not leave.

"You sure you don't want to go?" I said.

"Yep," he replied. Then he sat there, watching me. Watching watching watching.

I don't like it when people watch me. It makes me feel like I have a sign on my forehead that says, I AM REALLY WEIRD! PLEASE STARE AT ME! I needed to look busy so he would stop watching me, so I began to straighten up the secretary's desk. I picked up three papers and tapped them neatly together. I was very good at this, so I kept picking up papers and straightening them until all of the papers on the secretary's desk were in one neat stack. Underneath the papers was a folder. CHERRY HILL SPELLING BEE it said on the front, in bright red ink.

Oh my gosh! I thought. It was a folder about the spelling bee! I wondered what might be in there. A list of the class winners, a list of the judges, a list of the rules . . .

A list of the spelling bee words.

My insides exploded with tingles. I put my hand on the folder. I began to open it up.

"Are you supposed to be touching that?" the boy said.

I pulled my hand away from the folder. "Mr. Root told me to —"

"Go through those papers?" the boy said. "You're Sylvie Scruggs, right? You play baseball?"

"Maybe," I said, careful not to look amazed because he knew who I was. "How did you know?"

"I like baseball too," the boy said as if this answered my question. Then he just sat there, watching me again, a statue of jerkiness.

"What's *your* name?" I demanded.

"Daniel Fink." He leaned forward so he could see the folder. "Does that say *Spelling Bee?*"

"No!" I said, putting my hand over the words.

"Sylvie!" my mom shouted as she stomped into the office, a giggling Ginny on her hip. "Where are your brothers? What are you doing at that desk?"

"Sylvie!" Mr. Root said, flying into the room with Tate and Cale. "I've found your brothers — what are you doing at that desk?"

I slipped the folder underneath my neat stack of papers and hurried over to Tate and Cale, so everyone would remember that they were in big trouble, not me. The hurrying worked. "Boys!" my mom said. "You're covered in dirt! What's that in your hands?"

Tate held up a mess of sticks tangled up with string. "We were making this."

"It's a rabbit," Cale said. "He's our mascot. For our campaign."

"Mascot?" my mom said, looking at me with great suspicion.

"We named it Tree," Tate said. "Do you think the other kids will like it, Sylvie? We tried to build Tree a cage with some rusty old nails, but the cage fell apart."

"Because we didn't have any Popsicle sticks," Cale said.

"I found the boys in the bushes," Mr. Root explained. "They were finishing their creation and couldn't be bothered to go back to class."

"We didn't hear people calling our names," Tate said.

"We thought they were saying Pate and Gale," Cale said.

"And we don't know how we got in the bushes," Tate said.

Cale nodded. "It was an accident that Tate pushed me."

My mom sighed because my brothers are so hard.

"Wasn't Daniel in here?" Mr. Root said to me.

Surprised, I looked where Daniel Fink had been sitting, but he was gone. Mr. Root knew Daniel's name. This meant that either Daniel was Mr. Root's good friend, like me, or he was in trouble a lot.

"He must have left," Mr. Root said. "I'd better go check on him. Sylvie, I'll escort you back to class. Boys, I think you'd better go home with your mother. You are very dirty, even for kindergarteners."

"Yes," my mother said sadly. "I suppose they must come home. But, boys, you will hand me that thing you made. I don't want branches shedding all over my car."

"He's not a thing, he's Tree!" Cale said.

"He doesn't shed branches, he sheds carrots," Tate said.

As Mr. Root waved me out of his office, I looked longingly back at the secretary's desk. There it was, the spelling bee folder. It was practically begging for me to open it and find something to help Josh win. But unless there was a sudden earthquake and everyone ran from the room screaming, there was no way I could.

Chapter 6

When I got home from school that day, I called Josh.

"Are you still sick?" I said.

"Hi, Sylvie," Josh said in a croaky voice. "Yes, I'm sick. Stomach flu."

"That stinks," I said. "And I don't mean smells bad. I mean it *stinks* stinks."

"I know," Josh said.

"You mean, you know that it stinks or you knew what I meant?"

"Both," Josh said.

"Oh," I said.

Then we sat there for a while because I was trying to figure out something to say that would help Josh be healthy again, until Josh said, "What did you guys do at recess today?"

"Nothing," I said. "There's nothing to do if we don't play baseball. Most of the kids on the playground are too mean."

"Really?" Josh said.

"Yep," I said. Then I waited for him to figure out what I was trying to say without me having to say it. When he didn't, I said, "So, you know, it would probably be a good idea if you studied really hard."

"Okay," Josh said.

"Because it would probably be a good idea if you won the bee," I said.

"Okay," Josh said.

"We're going to have a pretend spelling bee at recess tomorrow to help you," I said.

"Okay," Josh said.

"It's important that you

do a good job so the other kids know how great you are."

"Okay," Josh said.

"You mean, 'Okay, I will study,' or 'Okay, I will win the bee'?"

"Okay, I will study," Josh said. "I don't know if I'll win the bee, but I'll try."

"Good," I said briskly, because this conversation had gone on long enough. "All you have to do is try. Try and win. I'll see you tomorrow."

"Okay," Josh said.

"But right now you should go study," I said. "Immediately. And probably for the rest of the night. Good-bye."

I hung up the phone and took a deep breath. *He'll do it,* I told myself. *The word* okay *basically means 'I promise,' and when Josh promises something, he does it. The end.*

Josh didn't come to school the next day.

"He's still sick," Alistair said when we met him on the sidewalk.

"No, he's not!" I said. "He promised he would come today!"

"He told you he was better?" Miranda said.

"He was going to come for our pretend bee!"

"He must have the weeklong flu," Alistair said in a wobbly voice. "He probably won't be better by Monday!"

I clamped my hand down on Alistair's shoulder to calm his panic, but panic was all that happened that day. Recess was even worse than the day before. We couldn't do the pretend bee without Josh, so we played group games in the outfield like stuck in the mud and Red Rover, the kind of games where the rules are always changing and people always get mad and everyone fights. They especially stink when fifth graders are watching you play them, and they are smirking and calling you a bunch of loser babies. Even worse, Daniel Fink was watching us from the trees *again*. Only this time, he knew my name and he knew I'd touched that spelling bee folder. He was the sad-looking boy who knew too much, and I didn't like it. Not one bit.

By the end of recess, my baseball friends were as lively as limp asparagus. The fifth graders were as triumphant as a herd of elephants. Something had to be done.

"We are still going to have our pretend spelling bee," I announced. "Only we'll do it at Josh's house."

"But he's sick," Miranda said.

Georgie elbowed me in the elbow and gestured toward the listening fifth graders. "He probably doesn't want *all* of us coming over to his house," he said.

"We *want* everyone to come," I whispered. "It's part of my plan."

"Great," Georgie said without any happiness in his voice. "You have a plan."

"Can we come too?" Giselle said.

I nodded. "Every one of us. Meet at Josh's house right after school."

"Maybe we should ask Josh first," Miranda whispered to me.

"I already told him about it on the phone," I explained. "I'm sure he'll want us to come."

After school that day, ten kids from our baseball team plus Miranda, Alistair, Georgie, and me walked to Josh's house. One of Josh's scary older sisters answered his door. Both of his sisters are in high school, and we never speak of them because they drive cars and wear makeup and talk really fast.

"What in the world?" she said as she chomped her gum and looked us over. "Josh is sick! Why are you here?"

None of us said anything, because it is not easy to say things to people who are chomping gum.

"Come back when he's better," she said after a gigantic eye roll that must have hurt with all that stuff on her eyelashes. She shut the door and we stood there, frozen, until we heard Josh's voice above our heads.

"Hey guys," he croaked. "What's going on?"

"He's up there!" Ezekiel shouted. "In the window."

We stepped away from the front door. Sure enough, there Josh was, leaning out an upstairs window. He looked a little sick. Okay, maybe a lot sick — green with dark circles under his eyes and a red nose and red eyeballs.

"You look awful!" Alistair shouted up at him. "Are you going to be able to spell on Monday?"

"We're here to have the real pretend spelling bee!" I shouted before Josh could answer that. "Can you come down?"

"No," Josh said in a wimpy voice. "I'm not allowed to play with anyone until we're sure I'm not contagious."

"That's a good idea!" Georgie shouted, because he is afraid of stomach flus. "Feel better, dude. See you later!"

That's when the munions arrived.

"Aren't you having the pretend bee?" munion number one said. "We wanted to help."

"Josh is too sick," Miranda began.

"We are having it," I told them. "We'll have it through the window. We can stay outside and Josh won't have to come down."

"Through the window?" Josh said.

"This is going to be hilarious," munion number one whispered loudly.

"I'm so glad we came," said munion number two.

Before they could say anything else incredibly rude, I began ordering everyone into position. Alistair and Georgie would be the judges, so I sat them on some large rocks in Josh's flower garden.

Miranda, as the word person, stood beneath the window. The rest of the kids — including the stupid munions who would not go away, even when I pointed out that we were having a way better pretend bee than theirs — sat down on the grass, because they were the audience. I climbed the tree nearest to Josh's window so I could be his coach and give him great spelling encouragement.

Once everyone was properly settled, I looked at Josh, then wished I hadn't. Josh really did look awful, as if he hadn't eaten for days. "Have you eaten for days?" I whispered so the audience couldn't hear me.

"I don't think so," he said, looking hungry and confused.

"Well, that's okay, because I'm your coach," I said to encourage him. "I can give you positive pep talks and help you with spelling strategies in between words. Though I can't tell you how to spell the words."

Josh put his hand to his forehead. He did some hard rubbing. "Okay," he said.

"Let the spelling bee begin!" I called with a
thumbs-up at Alistair, who was too busy staring at
Josh's greenness to notice.

Miranda was looking through the stack of
words our friends had collected for our pretend bee.
She frowned as if she didn't like most of them.
"*Hippopotamus!*" she called, giving Josh a toughie
right away.

"Um, let's see," Josh said, rubbing his ear.
"H-I-P — wait, did I already say *i*?"

"Yes," I said.

"*Ehhhhhhhhhh!*" Georgie shouted, making the sound of a gameshow buzzer. "No talking to the speller while they are spelling."

"But he asked a question!" I said.

"*Ehhhhhhhhhh!*" Georgie shouted again. "No questions in the middle of spelling."

"Georgie!" I called.

"He got it wrong!" someone whispered. "Oh no! He got *rhinoceros* wrong!"

"It was *hippopotamus*," munion number one said. "A word that everyone knows how to spell."

"That's okay," Miranda called. "Good try, Josh! Here's your next word: *diagonal*!"

Oh no! *Diagonal* was a really hard word. Maybe no one would notice if he spelled it wrong.

"D-I-E-A-H —" he began.

"*Ehhhhhhhhhh!*" Georgie shouted.

The munions laughed their horrible laughs.

"You're supposed to wait until he finishes the word!" I said to Georgie.

"That's a waste of time," Georgie said. "There is no *h* in diagonal, so I stopped him."

"We're supposed to be doing this like a real spelling bee," I said, trying to tell him with my stern eyebrows that he was ruining everything.

"Josh hasn't gotten any words right so far," Giselle said in her almost-crying voice.

"He's not going to," munion number two said.

"Here's another!" Miranda called. "*Fronds!*"

"*Fronds?*" Josh said, putting his elbows on the window and his head in his hands. "I've never even heard of that word. Is it French?"

Somebody groaned. The munions snorted like warthogs.

"Would you like a definition?" Miranda said. "You can always ask for a definition."

"Sure." Josh stretched his arm across the windowsill and laid his ear on it as if his neck was too tired to hold up his head.

"A big leaf that grows on a fern," Miranda said. "The kind of thing that waves in the breeze."

Josh didn't move. He didn't say any letters. He didn't do anything, probably because he had fallen asleep.

"*Ehhhhhhhhhh!*" Georgie shouted. "Time's up! Spell the word, Stetson."

"I didn't know there was a time limit on spelling!" Ezekiel said.

"Josh!" I whispered when he still didn't move. "Wake up! You need to spell *fronds!*"

Josh lifted his head and covered his eyes with both hands. "F-R-O-N-Z-E," he said.

Everyone looked at Miranda. Everyone held their breaths. I knew that was not how you spelled *fronds*. *Say* "correct" *anyway!* I thought at Miranda. *Pretend he got it right!*

"Incorrect," Miranda said.

Georgie opened his mouth to buzz, but Josh still had his hands over his eyes. Georgie looked at me instead. "This is stupid. Josh is too sick to spell."

"Come on, Josh!" I whispered. "You can do it. Just one word. Maybe *crescendo*. Could you spell *crescendo?*" The munions wouldn't know he already knew how to spell that word.

Josh dropped his head onto his arm and rolled it back and forth as if he were shaking his head no. "I gotta go," he whispered. His body slipped away from the window, his arms and hands disappearing last.

"Josh!" everyone shouted.

"Oh my gosh!" Giselle cried. "He's dead. Josh is dead!"

Josh stood up and darted away from the window like he had to get somewhere in a hurry. Probably to the bathroom. Probably to be sick.

"Where's he going?" Ezekiel called.

I jumped down from the tree. "Time to go," I said briskly. "He's just tired. He's been practicing really hard. Constantly. He's still a little sick, and when you're sick, it's impossible to spell correctly."

"Oh yeah," munion number one said with sarcasm dripping from her nostrils. "No one can ever spell when they're sick."

"But when they're not sick, they can suddenly remember everything!" munion number two said in the snottiest voice ever produced by a fifth grader. They stalked off together, their hair swishing. They seemed to be saying *Mission Accomplished. Josh stinks and everyone knows it.*

Oh, how I hated those munions! They didn't deserve to win! They deserved to lose and lose again and lose forever!

"We're never going to win," Giselle said before walking sadly in the direction of her house.

"We'll never play baseball again," Tiger and Ezekiel said before slumping off together.

Alistair just looked at me as if everything that had ever been wrong in the history of ever was my fault.

And, at that moment, I thought he was right.

Chapter 7

When I slumped into my house a few minutes later, my mom was waiting for me with a mommish smirk. "You have a letter," she said.

I looked at the small white envelope in her hand. "A letter?" I said. I'd never had a letter in my entire life except for every year at my birthday and two other times.

She handed it over. "The return address is in our neighborhood, but it doesn't say who it's from. There isn't a stamp, so I'm assuming it was hand delivered." She smirked her mommish smirk again. "Maybe it's an admirer."

I crossed my arms at her, because that was not funny. It was not only not funny, it was also stupid. Stupid and rude and inconsiderate and impolite and dumb. D-U-M-B.

"All right, all right!" she said after I said this two times. "I'm sorry. I'll go —" She paused to look at the envelope. "Unless — would you like me to watch you open it?"

I stared at my mother because she had gone completely crazy.

"Or maybe not," she said. Then she shut the door to leave me in my privacy.

I opened the envelope. The letter was written on very nice white paper with terrible handwriting that was almost impossible to read.

SYLVIE
i HAV SUMTHiN U
MyTE WANT
it HAZ 2 DUE
WITHH THE SpeLiN BEE.
IF U WANT iT, i WILL
CUMM 2 UR HOWS
2 MAHROW AFTERNOON
AT 4. I WILL
STAND BENEETH UR BiG
TREEE. DF
P.S. WRITE BACK iN CODE. OR YOU
CAN CALL ME NOT iN CODE
828-555-8841

It took me only three minutes (or maybe seven) to decipher this confusing letter. Someone wanted to give me something that had to do with the spelling bee, someone with the initials D. F. I only knew one person with those initials: Daniel Fink. The boy who watched me. He'd noticed the spelling bee folder too — he'd even asked me about it!

Oh my gosh! What if Daniel Fink had taken that spelling folder?

I stared at the letter for a long time, because there were two Sylvies having an elbow fight in my head. One Sylvie knew the truth: Josh could not spell when he was sick. Maybe he couldn't spell at all, and if he couldn't spell, we'd lose the field, and it would be all my fault. The other Sylvie knew the other truth: getting the spelling bee folder from Daniel Fink was a bad idea. I didn't know anything about him, and taking the folder might be cheating. Josh would not want to cheat. I did not want to cheat! Nobody wanted to cheat, except maybe Daniel Fink.

Two truths and no solution, unless —

I got out my special pen. I found paper every bit as nice as Daniel's and sat down to write.

DF, I wrote.

O.K. I WIL MEAT U ATT MY HOWSE 2MAHROW AT 4.

SS

I would meet him just to see what he had. It might not be the spelling bee folder, or it might be something that was not cheating but was helpful. Like a special medicine that would save Josh from the stomach flu. Meeting Daniel did not mean Josh was going to cheat, and if he just stared at me when he got here and said nothing, I could run inside my house and slam the door.

I sealed the letter up in an envelope, wrote *Daniel Fink* on the front with his address beneath, wrote my address in the left hand corner but *not* my name, because two can play at that game, and then I put the letter in our mailbox. Then I remembered that you have to put a stamp on the letter, so I ran out to get it, stuck on a stamp, and put the letter back in the mailbox. Then I remembered that I forgot to put the flag up on the mailbox, so I ran back out to put up the flag. Then my mom yelled at me for leaving the house again when it was time for dinner, so I couldn't run out one more time to make sure the stamp hadn't fallen off, but I stared at the mailbox through the window for five minutes to make sure no one stole the letter.

To my surprise, Daniel Fink limped out from a hiding spot in our neighbor's yard. He walked over to the mailbox, took my letter, then walked away.

Chapter 8

Josh did not come to school on Friday, because his mom said he was still recuperating, which reminded me of chickens, which is not a good thing to think about when you are trying to keep everyone happy. Miranda and Georgie were quiet and slumpy during class. Two kids got hurt while we were playing colored eggs at recess, and the recess monitor made everyone get off the field. Daniel Fink watched me from the trees again, like I was the weirdest person he'd ever seen.

"Can you play today?" Miranda said as we walked home.

I wish, I thought. *But I have to meet Daniel Fink all by myself in order to save the field.* "No," I said.

"So, what are we going to do if Josh is sick on Monday?" Georgie said.

I sighed and rubbed my cheekbones. "He's not going to be sick on Monday."

"I think we should tell the principal," Alistair said. "Maybe she'll put the spelling bee off for a week or two."

"Never tell principals anything," Georgie said.

"People don't stay sick on Mondays," I said with great firmness.

"Maybe one of us could pretend to be Josh," Alistair said, even though Miranda and I are girls, and all of us are shorter than Josh and different colors.

"Maybe Ms. Bloomen would let Miranda go in his place," Georgie said.

"I haven't been practicing!" Miranda said in alarm.

"But that would still be better than no one," Alistair said.

"We shouldn't tell Ms. Bloomen anything either," Georgie said.

"Would you all just stop!" I said. Okay, shouted.

"Josh is not going to be sick, he will win the spelling bee, and we will keep our baseball field! Everything is going to be fine!"

"Then why are you shouting?" Alistair said.

When I got home, I found my brothers in the kitchen again, eating carrots and celery and cabbage.

"Tate thinks eating rabbit food will give us magic powers to change the vote," Cale said as he nibbled on a giant leaf.

Tate was not eating the vegetables. He was stealing bites from a cookie he was hiding under the table. "It's our only hope to win," he said. "Our campaign has been shut down."

"Shut down?" I said.

"Mr. Takaru made us throw away our posters," Tate explained.

"But posters are a great idea!" I said. "Why did he make you throw them away?"

A tear ran down Cale's cheek. It was followed by a million more. "He said we can't hang bloody lizards on our desks, because there would be nightmares at nap time."

"You drew bloody lizards?" I said.

"Green is so boring!" Cale cried. "Our posters needed more colors."

Tate pounded his fist on the table. "The rabbit we drew ate the lizards only *after* they were dead."

"The lizards were squished by cars," Cale explained. "Tree wouldn't eat alive lizards."

"Did you tell that to your teacher?" I said.

Cale shook his head. "He wouldn't even listen!"

"Not even after I called him a lizard!" Tate said.

I closed my eyes. I wished that when my eyes opened, my brothers wouldn't be so difficult, but when I opened them, they still were. I felt sorry for Tate and Cale, but they needed to take this rabbit problem into their own hands. "You'll have to go underground," I told them firmly. "You have to take this campaign to the people."

"Under the ground?" Tate said.

"Undercover," I explained, trying to remember the words my dad used when he talked about running for student representative. "A whisper campaign."

"We should whisper to people under the covers?" Cale said.

I looked out the window at my front yard, where Daniel Fink would appear any minute. "Sometimes you have to do things you wouldn't normally do so people don't get mad at you and nobody is sad.

That's why you have to whisper," I said. "So things stay secret."

"Secret?" my brothers said. "What secret?"

I thought of spelling folders. I thought of spelling lists. "I'll explain more later. Right now, I need your help, and it will have to be a secret."

"I don't like secrets," Cale said. "Because when I tell them on accident, I get really sad."

"Why do we have to be a secret?" Tate said.

I spotted some bushes at the side of the house that would be perfect for my brothers. "Because you're going undercover," I said.

Five minutes later, my brothers were hiding like good magic bunnies in the bushes. "You stay right where you are and listen carefully," I told them. "A big and staring fifth grader named Daniel Fink is coming over. He thinks I'm weird."

"Yes," Tate said, as if he agreed with Daniel Fink.

"That's Mary Fink's robot brother!" Cale said.

"Daniel Fink is not a robot," I said. "You shouldn't listen to those evil munions!"

"We didn't listen to those evil munions," Tate said. "We hate them, like you told us to. Mary told us about her brother. He's not a *whole* robot, he's just part of a robot. He's got a robot leg."

"I don't like Mary Fink," Cale said. "Even if she does have a robot brother. She wants the class pet to be a lizard."

I sighed, because I didn't have time for a lecture, but my brothers needed one right away. "Even if you don't like someone, you need to find a way of getting along with them," I said. "And if you can't agree about something, you need to find a way to share. The end."

"We can't share," Tate said, his little hands on his little hips. "You can't have half a lizard and half a rabbit. That would be a lizbit!"

"Or a razard," Cale said. "And the rabbit part would want to jump while the lizard part would slither! Slither-jump, slither-jump — it wouldn't work!"

"Of course that wouldn't work," I told them as I struggled with all my brains to think of a way they could share the class pet. But it was just like the baseball field. Mary Fink and the rest of their class wanted a lizard. Tate and Cale wanted a rabbit. We wanted the field every day. The fifth graders wanted the field every day. There was no way to share, and I refused to share with those munions anyway. Over my dead baseball body.

"*Psst! Psst!*" Cale practically shouted. "Giant boy alert! Giant boy alert!"

"He's heading this way!" Tate cried. "All magic bunnies into the bunny hole!"

"We're already in the hole," Cale said. "Except it's not a hole, it's a bush."

"Be quiet!" I hissed at them. "You are here for my protection!" I turned around to face Daniel Fink. He was even bigger on my lawn, especially because he was wearing fancy black pants and shiny shoes and a white shirt and tie.

"Did you just come from church?" I said.

Daniel shook his head.

"A wedding?"

He shook his head again.

"A cookie festival?" Tate asked from his spot in the bushes.

Daniel looked at the bushes, where you could see my brothers perfectly because they are so bad at hiding. "No," he said.

To distract him from Tate and Cale, I thrust out something I'd put together for him last night. It was triple-wrapped in plastic grocery bags. "Here," I said.

Daniel took it from my hand as if it might be elephant poop.

I lowered my voice so my brothers wouldn't hear. "That's payment," I said. "So you'll give me the folder with no shoelaces attached."

"The folder?" Daniel said.

I sighed in frustration, because Daniel had been standing on my grass for practically lots of minutes. These sorts of deals were supposed to be quick so no one spotted them. "The spelling bee folder on the school secretary's desk!" I hissed. "You have it, right?"

"I — I don't have a folder." Daniel tucked my triple-wrapped package under his arm while he fished a wad of something out of his pocket.

"Don't squeeze those too hard," I warned him, pointing at my package. "They can be delicate."

"What are they?" he said.

"Jelly beans," I whispered so my brothers couldn't hear. "Two hundred different flavors. My entire collection."

"You're giving him your jelly beans?" Tate cried.

Cale gasped. "Not the coconuts!"

Daniel paused to look at the package. "Two hundred different flavors?" he said.

"Almost," I said. "One hundred and four." Then I held out my hand and waited for him to give me the wad of what looked like folded-up paper. "What is this?"

Daniel dangled it over my palm. "It's the spelling bee word list," he said.

"The list?" My head and legs went tingly. "I don't really want the list. I mean, I *do* want the list, but I also don't. I don't want it so Josh can cheat. No sirree, Bobby. Josh is not a cheater. He is anticheating."

Daniel said nothing.

"Josh is not going to cheat," I continued. "Not not not. Most definitely not. He doesn't even know about the list. I just thought it might be interesting to see what *kinds* of words they would use in a school bee."

Daniel still said nothing because he never speaks.

"I will not quiz Josh on this list," I went on. "I will not. Nope! I probably won't even look at the list myself. Well, maybe I'll look at it. But not to cheat! Because we are not cheaters. Josh would never cheat on purpose. But he's been really sick."

"Is it okay to cheat when you're sick?" Cale asked Tate.

"If Sylvie says it is," Tate whispered. "But that's probably why we are a secret."

"So do you want the list?" Daniel said after glancing at my loud and obvious brothers who were never going to get coconut jelly beans from me again.

"Yes," I said.

But instead of giving me the list, he put down my jelly bean package and got down on one knee. He placed the wad of paper on the palm of his hand. He held it out to me like a waiter holding out his tray of food. "You can have it," he said with a croak. "But you'll have to be my girlfriend."

The sky went dark. Thunder clouds clapped. A lion roared far away in a jungle. Okay, not really, but it seemed like it, because Daniel Fink had not just said what I thought he'd said. "Your girlfriend!" was all I could say.

"I don't like jelly beans," Daniel said. "And you like baseball. Plus, you're not like those other stupid

girls." He looked at me as if he meant every word he'd just said.

"I can't be your girlfriend!" I cried.

Daniel frowned. "You *can*," he said. "Anyone could if they wanted to."

"But I *don't* want to!" I said.

"Yeah," Cale shouted. "Leave her alone! She doesn't want to be your pinecone!"

"He said *girlfriend*, not *pinecone*," Tate whispered. "*Pinecone* is worse."

"Should we call 911?" Cale said.

"Probably," Tate said.

"Nine one one!" they both shouted at the top of their lungs.

"I can help you win that rabbit," Daniel said to them.

They immediately stopped shouting.

"You're in kindergarten with my sister, Mary, right? She says the lizard is going to win for sure."

Cale and Tate looked at each other like desperate magic bunnies. "How would you help us?" Cale said.

"Will it be a secret?" Tate said. "Because I've been a little sick, so it's okay."

"Boys!" I cried. "Go into the house this instant!"

Tate crawled out of the bushes and Cale followed. "What would you do?" Tate said to Daniel, ignoring my orders.

"Would it hurt?" Cale whispered, wincing as if it already did.

"I'll pay you for the list," I told Daniel. "I have five dollars I can give you right now. But I won't be your girlfriend!"

"What does *girlfriend* mean?" Tate said.

Cale walked up beside me. "Will she have to hold your hand?"

Daniel shook his head. "Gross."

"What about hugs?" Tate said. "Will she have to do that? Because Nathan and Ellie in our class always hug and they are boyfriend/girlfriend."

Daniel shuddered. "No."

"You don't want her to kiss you, do you?" Cale said.

"No!" Daniel and I both shouted.

"Then what does she have to do?" Tate said.

"Sit with me at lunch," Daniel said as if he'd thought about this a lot. "And hang out with me at recess. Stand by me whenever we're in the same place, and sit by me at assemblies."

"That's it?" Tate said. "That's easy! That's just like being a friend."

"Except it's being a girlfriend!" I said.

"You know Josh is going to lose if you don't give him the list," Daniel said.

I gulped, because it was true.

Daniel looked at my brothers. "I'll make sure they get the rabbit for no extra charge."

"How long do I have to be your girlfriend?" I whispered, because if he said forever, I would probably die. Right there. On my front lawn.

"For the rest of the year," Daniel said, which was pretty much forever. He still held the wad of paper out in front of me. "Is it a deal?"

Josh was going to lose the spelling bee, and then we would lose the field. Sixteen people would have nothing to do at recess because they didn't fit in anywhere else. Those munions would win, and everyone would blame the great spelling bee disaster on me, Sylvie Scruggs. I could fix that. I could fix that right now just by being Daniel Fink's girlfriend for three months.

Three whole months.

But Josh *might* win the spelling bee if he got better. There was a small, tiny, tiny chance. And if he didn't win, it would be okay. A terrible cyclone wouldn't destroy the earth and toss us into space forever. We could learn how to play soccer and hopscotch and king of the playground mountain. It would be awful and boring and the worst thing ever, but we could do it. And I didn't want to cheat. I never wanted to cheat.

"No," I said.

Chapter 9

After Daniel left, Cale started crying. "Did you see how sad he looked? He wanted you to marry him!" He threw his arms around me and blew his nose on my shirt.

Tate kicked me in the leg, but not too hard. "You were going to cheat for the spelling bee, and I really wanted a rabbit!" Then he ran inside the house and shut the door.

"I'm sorry Josh is going to lose," Cale said.

I sighed and nodded. I felt so sad inside, I couldn't speak. I could think of only one thing we could do. "Josh is very sick," I told Cale. "He needs to get better so he can spell. Let's go make him some soup."

We hurried to the kitchen and opened up three cans of cream of mushroom soup that were very old and dusty on the outside. We poured them into a pot.

"That looks like gray jelly with gray blobs," Cale said.

I looked at the blobs in the pot. They needed work, but there wasn't time. "Let's put them in a Tupperware," I said. "Then we can put it in the microwave with the lid on it. That way, we won't know what it looks like when it's done."

Cale thought this was a great plan, so we put the lid on the Tupperware, then put it in the microwave for ten minutes. Cale left then because ten minutes is a long time when you're small, and when the time was up, I took out the Tupperware and wrapped it in a cloth because it was boiling hot. I was heading out the front door when Miranda appeared.

"Hi!" she said.

"Oh, good," I said. "You're here. I need to go to Josh's, and I don't want to go by myself."

Miranda let me take her hand and lead her toward the sidewalk. "Why?" she said.

I looked down at my nourishing soup hidden inside the towels. Miranda might not like this idea. She might say that someone with the stomach flu probably shouldn't eat. "I'll tell you later," I said. Then I moved even faster.

When we got to Josh's front door, Miranda pointed to my Tupperware. "Something's leaking out the bottom."

She was right. The Tupperware was dripping gray slime onto the sidewalk. I tossed the whole thing into the bushes by the porch just as the door opened.

It was Josh's mom. "Girls!" she exclaimed. "So good to see you! Josh isn't here. He's running an errand with his older sister, but they should be back soon. Would you like to come in? I have some bear claws left over from a work meeting, and I can pour you a glass of milk."

Miranda and I looked at each other because we had never eaten bear claws before. They sounded really gross, even if they were cooked in butter, but Miranda was interested, because she is a scientist.

"That would be very nice," she said superpolitely. "Thank you."

"But we don't have to eat the bear claws," I said as we walked into the kitchen. "Because Josh might want to eat them if he's feeling better. Is he feeling better?"

"He's feeling so much better," Mrs. Stetson said. "And he loves bear claws. That's why I want you to eat some. If he gets his hands on them after not eating for days, he'll make himself sick!"

I glanced at Miranda in alarm. She looked worried too. "I'm allergic —" I began, but Mrs. Stetson interrupted me.

"Truthfully, I'm glad you've come when Josh is

out." She gestured to some seats at the kitchen table, then walked over to a box on the counter. She began pulling giant pastries from the box and setting them on plates. I searched her kitchen with my eyes for any sign of bear claws, but saw nothing. "I've been wanting to thank you for months now," Mrs. Stetson said.

Miranda took a seat next to me. "Thank us?"

"For befriending Josh this year! You know, he's always been shy and never had a lot of friends. I'm so grateful that Georgie moved into the neighborhood and you four found each other." Mrs. Stetson brought us each a pastry and a glass of milk, then took a seat beside me.

Miranda sniffed at her pastry to check for bear claws. "We're glad we found Josh too."

Mrs. Stetson beamed. "Josh has gained so much confidence recently. Playing on that hockey team was the first organized sport he's ever done. Then he became team captain! Now, he's convinced he's going to win this spelling bee. It's all he talked about when he wasn't throwing up. Spelling bee this, spelling bee that. He's been studying so hard!"

"Really?" Miranda said. We looked at each other, dread on our faces. Josh couldn't spell *hippopotamus* or *diagonal* or *fronds*. His studying hadn't worked!

"We've gone over list after list!" Mrs. Stetson had a pastry in her hand as if she was about to eat it, but she suddenly dropped it back onto her plate. "Here, I'll show you," she said. She ushered us upstairs to Josh's bedroom. It was a perfectly clean room with a nicely made bed, an organized desk, and an alphabetized bookshelf. The turtle tank where Josh kept Mr. Crispy, his turtle, sat against the wall. His hockey equipment was neatly arranged on the floor near his chest of drawers.

None of that was a surprise. Josh was the sort of person who would keep everything neat and tidy. What surprised me were the words — lists and lists of them all over the walls, on the back of his door,

and on the sides of his furniture. Some of the lists were handwritten, some were typed. All of them had been underlined or highlighted as if he'd studied every single word in this room, which had to be millions of words.

"Oh my goodness!" Miranda cried. "He's been working so hard!"

Mrs. Stetson nodded proudly. "He told me he'd promised Sylvie that he wasn't going to give up, so he didn't! I do hope he wins — I'm afraid he'll be crushed if he doesn't. But he'll have you to support him no matter what, right?"

"Right!" Miranda said.

"Right," I whispered, because I'd created a spelling monster. Josh had studied so hard, he would nearly die if he lost! This was all my fault. If I hadn't insisted that he practice, he probably wouldn't have studied at all!

"He wants to have you over tomorrow afternoon for spelling bee practice. I'm going to make treats.

Oh, that's the garage. He must be home! Quick!" Mrs. Stetson ushered us into the hallway. "He'd be so embarrassed if he knew I showed you his lists. Let's keep this a secret, okay?"

A secret. Another secret. "I have to go," I said, hurrying not to the kitchen, where the pastries and the bear claws and Josh would be waiting, but to the front door. "We need to hurry home, right, Miranda?"

"But your bear claws!" Mrs. Stetson said. "You haven't finished them."

"That's okay, because I'm allergic to dead animal parts," I said. "But the pastries were delicious. Tell Josh not to worry about the spelling bee because he's totally going to win. One hundred percent."

Miranda and I practically ran out the front door.

"Did you see those walls?" Miranda whispered as we fled. "All those words! And he was still having a hard time spelling the other day. What if he loses?"

"He's not going to lose," I said.

"He might," she said. "You don't know that for sure."

"Yes, I do know that," I said as I pictured Daniel Fink kneeling down on one knee. "I really do."

When I got home, I pulled out Daniel Fink's letter. I dialed his phone number.

Daniel answered. "Hello," he said.

"This is Sylvie," I said.

"I know," Daniel said. "Do you want the list?"

"Yes," I said.

"Are you there?" Daniel said, because I hadn't actually said the word out loud.

"Yes," I said out loud.

"And you'll be my girlfriend?"

"Yes," I said, all the way out loud so he wouldn't ask it again.

"You will?" Daniel said. "Oh boy, that's great. That's really great. Thanks, Sylvie! You'll sit by me at the spelling bee, right?"

Relief poured over me like a gigantic waterfall. At least I didn't have to do that. "We have to sit with our classes at assemblies," I reminded him.

"Oh yeah," Daniel said. "But you'll stand by me at recess?"

"Yes," I whispered.

"And you'll sit by me at lunch?"

"Yes," I whispered again.

"Great!" he shouted. "I can't wait. I thought you might change your mind, so I left the list in your mailbox under a rock. And I'll make sure your brothers win the rabbit vote too. See you Monday!"

I hung up the phone. I forced myself out of my room, down the hall, out of my house, and to the mailbox. There it was. Under a rock. The wad of paper. The list.

One minute later, I knocked on Miranda's door.

"Hi!" she said. "Oh my gosh, what's the matter?"

I handed her the paper, which I hadn't even opened. "Will you give this list to Josh for me tomorrow? It's a really important list of spelling words. Good ones. He should memorize them."

"Aren't you coming to the pretend spelling bee tomorrow?" Miranda said. "Why do you look so sad? Have you been crying?"

"I have an allergy to bear claws," I explained, rubbing my eyes. "So I'm going to stay home. Just give Josh the list, okay?"

Miranda nodded. "Okay. But where did you get it?"

"Bye," I said, as if I had somewhere important

to go, which I did. I needed to go into my room and climb into my bed and pretend like I hadn't just promised to be Daniel Fink's girlfriend and made Josh a cheater. Except that's exactly what I'd done.

Chapter 10

I stayed home on Saturday and organized our basement all by myself, because there might be spiders in the basement and you can't think about cheating or boyfriends when you're worried about spiders. On Sunday, I went to church, then came home and tried to teach Ginny how to crawl, because it takes a lot of focus to teach a baby how to crawl. Then I went to bed early and imagined that Monday would never come. Maybe when I woke up, magically, *amazingly*, it would be Sunday again.

But Monday came anyway, even though I kept my eyes shut as long as possible when my alarm went off.

"Good morning, Sylvie!" my dad said as he pranced around my room, putting laundry away.

I groaned and put a pillow on top of one ear so I

wouldn't hear him. Daniel had probably already made me a necklace that said *Daniel Fink's Girlfriend.* I groaned again and pressed the pillow down on my face.

"Having a hard time waking up?" my dad said.

I sat up to frown at him. "Why would a person have a robot leg?"

My dad stopped prancing. "Do you mean Daniel Fink?"

My mouth fell open, because, somehow, my dad had become a genius. "How did you know?" I said.

"I ran into his mother at Cherry Hill last week, and she told me about Daniel," he explained. "A little over a year ago, he got bone cancer." He bent over to put my shirts in the shirt drawer. "The cancer became so advanced, they had to amputate one of his legs below the knee."

"Amputate!" I said. "Like cut off?"

Dad shut my shirt drawer. "That's what *amputate* means. He limps because he has a prosthetic leg. He used to be a champion baseball player too, poor kid. I'm glad you're becoming friends with him. The fifth graders at your school haven't been too kind, according to his mother. Hey, isn't the big spelling bee today?"

I nodded, or at least I think I nodded. I was still thinking about Daniel's leg being cut off. I couldn't even imagine how much that would hurt!

"I think your mom is going to come watch if Ginny cooperates. She'd like to support Josh. Sylvie?" My dad paused to squint his eyes at me. "Your eyes are red — are you all right?"

"Sylvie?" Miranda said an hour later as we walked into our cafetorium. "Are you all right?"

"I'm fine," I said, which was the biggest lie of my life. "Quick, let's sit down!" I wanted to find a spot before Daniel entered the room and waved his arms at me and cried, "Hi, girlfriend!"

We sat down as fast as we could, Georgie on my right, Miranda on my left, but it didn't help. Daniel's class filed in right behind us. "Sylvie!" he said as he sat down in the row behind me. "We're almost sitting together, right?"

"Wait, do you know each other?" munion number one said. She was three people to the left of Daniel. She looked at his beaming face. She looked at my red one. Then she whispered something to Jamie Redmond and three other girls near her, who exploded with laughter. Jamie just tilted her head and looked at me funny.

Luckily, everyone began clapping then, because

Josh and munion number two and the other class champions had just entered the cafetorium, heading for the stage. A little girl who looked exactly like Daniel was one of the champions. *That must be Mary Fink!* I thought. Maybe Daniel had given her the words too!

Josh had to be at Cherry Hill a little early to meet with the principal, so Miranda and Georgie and I hadn't seen him yet. He looked extra-thin and extra-pale, but at least he wasn't green. He scanned the room until he found us. Then his whole face lit up as if we were electricity and he was a lightbulb.

Miranda waved at him with great cheerfulness. "That was a great list you gave me for Josh," she whispered. "The words were really interesting. He memorized them so quickly!"

"He memorized all of them?" I said. "Every single one?" But Miranda didn't answer, because Josh was waving at someone and she turned around to see who. It was his mother, Mrs. Stetson. She sat in the front row of the grown-ups, who were behind all the kids. My mom sat beside her with Ginny in her lap. Next to my mom was a real live policewoman.

I turned around as fast as I could. I took a deep breath. *It's okay,* I told myself. *It's just a police officer, not a monster. She's probably here to watch for cheating, but since Josh didn't cheat, she won't catch him.*

"Want to sit by your boyfriend, Scruggs?" munion number one whispered.

"Some of the words you gave us were so weird," Miranda was saying. "*Extraterritorial,* for example. I had to look it up in the dictionary, but you were right! It was a word!"

"Shhh!" I said to Miranda, because if she kept saying the words out loud, someone would hear her, and they'd know she'd seen the words beforehand.

Oh my gosh! I thought as a blanket of dread whacked me in the face. Miranda would recognize the words in the bee. She'd know we cheated, and she'd be furious!

"Maybe we should go to the bathroom," I whispered.

"No, silly!" she said. "The bee's about to start. Cross your fingers for Josh!"

"Cross your fingers for the baseball field," Georgie said.

"Is that all you can think about at a time like this?" I demanded.

"Students of Cherry Hill Elementary, BE QUIET!" Principal Stoddard shouted into the microphone. Screechy sounds bounced around the cafetorium. Everyone put their hands over their ears except for me. I was too busy thinking of a way to get Miranda and Josh out of the room so they wouldn't hear the spelling words. Except Josh would have to hear the spelling words, because he would have to spell them.

"Scruggs and Robot Leg," munion number one whispered. "*So happy together!*"

"Don't call him Robot Leg!" I whispered. Okay, not exactly whispered. I glanced at the police officer, then glanced away. I couldn't let her get a good look at me.

A tiny boy walked to the podium. He grabbed the microphone with both hands. Then he fell over, taking the microphone down with him. His arms and legs got tangled up in the cords. Principal Stoddard got the boy standing up again and helped him adjust the microphone. The boy looked at the policewoman and fell over again.

"Josh is trying to smile at you," Miranda said. "Look at him, Sylvie!"

But I couldn't, so I squeezed Miranda's knee so she would be quiet and maybe have to go to the bathroom.

When the boy was finally upright, one of the judges said the word *drummer*, and the first round began. It was full of easy words like *sandwich*, *forget*, *turnip*, and *whaling*. Every time a judge said a word, I glanced at Miranda to see if she recognized it, but her face stayed the same. Alert, like a giraffe. Josh got the word *patient*, which, thank goodness, he would have spelled correctly anyway. Maybe all of Josh's words would be easy words he'd known before I gave him the list. Then he wouldn't be cheating!

In the second round, Josh spelled *typically* correctly. "Josh knew that word a long time ago, right?" I asked Miranda.

She looked at me, not smiling. Her forehead was crunched. She looked confused, as if she was thinking too hard about spelling words. "Never mind!" I whispered.

The bee went on. Rounds three, four, and five passed by. Josh spelled *triumphant, remorseful,* and *tremendous.*

"Josh is getting really easy words, right?" I said to Georgie, who elbowed me in the elbow.

Round six began with no kindergarteners, first graders, or second graders left, including Mary Fink. Daniel must not have given her the words, even though he had them. I was so sweaty, my hands wouldn't stay dry no matter how much I wiped them on my pants. Mrs. Stetson looked proud, like Josh had just brought home one hundred of her favorite bear claws. Would she look that happy if she knew Josh had cheated?

When round eleven began, there were only four spellers left: Josh, munion number two, and the other two fifth graders. The rest of the fourth graders were out. Josh was our last chance.

"*Perpendiculars*," the judge said to Josh.

"Shoot!" I whispered, because that was a hard word. Josh might not have known that word before. I looked at Miranda to see what she thought, but she was staring at Josh and biting her lip.

"P," he said slowly, "E–R–P–E–N–D–I–C–U —" Josh stopped. He shut his mouth. He turned red, which made me wonder if he was still breathing.

Get it wrong! I thought. *Get it wrong so you don't cheat!*

"L–A–R," Josh said as the crowd held their breaths. "S," he added at last, and everyone sighed in relief. Except for me.

When round twelve began, only Josh and munion number two were left.

"We are so totally going to win," munion number one whispered to my back. "Then you won't be able to play baseball ever again."

"Josh has totally got this!" Georgie whispered to her. "The field is going to be ours!"

I looked at Georgie to see if he actually *knew* Josh would win because he knew that Josh had already learned these words. Georgie's eyes were shining. His nostrils were flexed. He sure looked like he knew something, but he didn't look unhappy about it. Maybe he didn't care if Josh had to cheat to win.

I looked back at Daniel Fink. He shook his head at me as if he was trying to tell me something.

"*Exorcise*," the judge said to the munion.

She spelled it correctly.

"*Extraterrestrial*," the judge said to Josh.

Oh no! I thought. *That was the word Miranda said earlier!*

"E," Josh began.

I looked up. Josh looked stressed, as if he'd just realized he was cheating, and he didn't want the letters to come. He was not a cheating person. He'd never forgive himself if he cheated.

"X-T-R-A-T-E-R-R-E-S-T-R-I-A-L," Josh said, finishing fast.

"Correct!" the judge cried.

"No!" I shouted, jumping to my feet. "It's cheating! Give him another word! One that's not on that list!"

No one moved, no one made a sound. Josh looked right at me, shocked. Then he took a step back, and the cafetorium exploded like a den of roaring lions. Kids whispered, talked, and shouted. Others laughed so hard, they snorted, mostly the fifth graders. Way up front, still sitting in his row, Cale was crying. Tate put his hands over Cale's mouth to shut him up, but that only made him cry harder.

"It wasn't Josh's fault!" I called over the noise. "It was my fault. I gave him the word list!"

"Shut up, Sylvie!" Georgie said. "Josh was about to win!"

"Quiet, all of you!" Principal Stoddard thundered into the microphone. "I want inside voices now!"

She didn't get them. The judges were talking to her, shaking their heads. The police officer was approaching the stage, heading toward Josh.

Oh no! I thought. *The police officer is going to arrest Josh!*

Cale nearly knocked me over as he ran like a

leopard to our mom. "It wasn't the rabbit!" he wailed. "It was the lizard. The lizard!"

Tate chased after him, screaming, "Stop in the name of the magic bunny!"

Everyone was standing now. Daniel Fink came up to me. "Josh didn't cheat," he whispered. "And you don't have to be my girlfriend."

The munions surrounded us. "Josh cheated, so we win!" munion number two said.

"So Robot Leg *is* your boyfriend?" munion number one said.

"Don't call him Robot Leg!" I shouted.

"Sylvie Scruggs!" Mr. Root boomed into the microphone.

The room went still. Up on the stage, Mr. Root stood with one hand on Josh's shoulder. Josh stared at his feet. He looked as if I'd just punched him in the stomach with sixteen different elbows. Mr. Root stepped away from the microphone. "In my office. Immediately."

My mom followed me into the
office with Ginny on her
hip and Cale sobbing
at her side. Tate
came in behind
Cale, looking like
he wanted to bite
him in the ankle.
Mr. Takaru, their
teacher, walked in
after them. He looked
as if his kindergarten-
ers had bitten him in
the ankle one hundred
times. Mrs. Stetson and
Josh were there already.

The police officer entered last with Mary Fink and Daniel.

The office was crowded. Mr. Root ran his fingers through the hair he didn't have and suggested that my mom take the sobbing Cale and go home. I thought this was a great idea, because I didn't want my mom or my brothers to be in the room when I confessed to cheating, but my mom shook her head.

"I'd like to stay with Sylvie, if you don't mind," she said. "And I know this isn't the time, but Cale is going to have a heart attack if he doesn't confess something he seems to think is very important."

Everyone looked at Cale. "We we we —" he began before bursting into a round of goopy sniffles and snorts.

"We cheated," Tate said, rubbing at the carpet with his foot. "We put extra votes in the box so we could get a rabbit for a class pet. Because we've always wanted one."

"Ah!" Mr. Takaru said. "That explains why there were sixty-four papers in the box."

"Cale!" my mom said. "Tate! How could you?"

"It was my idea," Daniel said, stepping forward, his right foot landing with a thump. "I told them what to do and how to do it. I even made the extra voting slips."

"Daniel!" his sister cried. "You were supposed to help me get a lizard!"

"That's the interesting thing," Mr. Takaru said. "There were sixty-four votes in the box. Thirty-two of them were for the rabbit, and thirty-two were for the lizard. Someone arranged things so that no one would lose."

Daniel nodded, but did not explain. Then he took a deep breath. "The list I gave Sylvie wasn't real. I made it up, so Josh didn't really cheat."

"You made it up?" I said. "You mean, you didn't get it from the folder?"

Daniel shook his shaggy head, his eyes on the ground.

"What list?" Josh said.

"What list?" my mom said.

"The spelling list," Cale said. "But it's a secret."

"Daniel Fink!" the police officer, who must have been Daniel and Mary's mom, said.

"But *I* voted for the rabbit because I felt sorry for you!" Mary said to my brothers. "There should have been one extra vote for the rabbit."

"No," Cale sniffled. "Because I voted for the lizard. So we wouldn't be cheating so much."

Mr. Root took control of the situation. "Daniel, you and your mother wait out here, please. I'd like to see Sylvie and Mrs. Scruggs and Josh and Mrs. Stetson in my private office. Mr. Takaru, please take your students back to class. Perhaps you can have another vote?"

Mr. Takaru looked at the hysterical Cale. "If you three can calm down, you will find, when we return, that a nice compromise has already been made."

"It has?" Tate said with a huge chunk of suspicion.

"Are you going to give us money?" Mary Fink said through her tears. "Because I'd like five bucks."

It took a long time for me to explain everything. I had to start at the baseball field and the sadness of my team, and end with the spelling bee and how I was a big fat cheater. So much had happened in between that when you told the whole story at once, it sounded really, really bad. I didn't say anything about Josh or his mom or the lists on his walls, because those were supposed to stay a secret.

"Sylvie," Mr. Root said when I was finished, "I don't believe, in my ten years as assistant principal, I've ever heard of someone with better intentions making such enormous mistakes. It's clear that you were trying to save your baseball field for the kids who needed it. It's also clear that you allowed yourself to forget what was right and wrong along the way."

"Yes," my mom said as she helped Ginny with a burp. "Amen."

"You should have given Josh a chance to win the spelling bee without cheating," Mr. Root said. "He is an excellent speller, as he proved today. He knew all of those words without any help from you."

I looked at Josh. His head was down and he was staring at his hands.

"I wasn't sure," I said. "I mean, I didn't know. He'd been so sick." I stopped talking then, because everything I said made it sound as if I hadn't thought Josh could win. Which was true. I hadn't.

"You need to have more faith in your friends," Mr. Root said.

"I think," Mrs. Stetson said slowly, "that even when you do have faith in someone, it's hard to leave winning to chance. Because you know that person wants to win so much." She looked at me. "Is that right, Sylvie?"

Tears were in my eyeballs. I sniffed and wiped at my nose so they would go away. "Yes," I said. "I'm sorry."

Mr. Root stood up, his jolly face lost in the wrinkles on his forehead. "Sylvie, you and Daniel both demonstrated that you will do almost anything for your friends — or your lack of friends. But some things are more important than even friendship. Things like honesty. Do you understand?"

I nodded, even though I was pretty sure I didn't want to understand anything ever again. It hurt too much.

Mr. Root's jolly face returned. "Now, according to the judges, the interruption was the sort that necessitates either starting over completely or allowing for a tie, and we are *not* starting over again. So Josh and Alexa have tied for first place. I'm afraid, Sylvie, you'll have to think of another way to solve the baseball field problem. I sympathize with those kids who have nothing else to do, but if you can't work things out" — he paused and waited until all eyes were on him — "we may have to ban baseball for the rest of the year."

Mr. Root dismissed us. He said Josh and I could go home for the rest of the day, but we would have to return to school tomorrow.

"Mr. Root?" I said as I walked out of his office. "Maybe you shouldn't punish Daniel. He wouldn't have done anything if I hadn't asked him to."

Mr. Root smiled a quiet smile. "Thank you, Sylvie. Daniel's had a rough time of it ever since he moved here. He's had a rough time of things for several years. I think he'd do just about anything to make a friend." He paused to give me a grown-up, important look. "Maybe now, he won't have to."

On our way to the parking lot, Mrs. Stetson and my mom began talking about how hard it is to raise children in this day and age, and they forgot all about Josh and me as we walked behind them. This was good and bad. I was happy to be forgotten by my mom, but I didn't want to be walking alone with Josh. I wanted to crawl into my bed and put my pillow over my face and pretend that I was in third grade again, when life had been simple.

I knew that Josh would never get mad at me. We'd just go on being brisk and smiling friends, and we'd pretend for the rest of forever that none of this had ever happened. Only it had happened, and even if Josh forgot about it, I never would.

"I'm sorry," I whispered in my most whispering voice. "I shouldn't have done that. Not without asking — only I knew you wouldn't want to cheat, and I didn't know how smart you'd become at spelling. I was worried about you. I didn't want you to lose! I was worried about the baseball field. I was worried about our team and that I'd messed everything up. So I was stupid. Extra-stupid."

Josh nodded. "I would rather lose than cheat. Winning's not that important to me, but I know it's important to you. Especially when it's against those munions."

I looked at Josh, astonished. Winning wasn't that important to me! Not really. Not exactly. I was worried about the baseball kids and about Josh and Alistair and the field. I didn't care about those munions at all. Did I?

A new truth whacked me right in the face. Josh was right. I *had* been worried about the field and about Josh and my team and everything else, but I'd also really wanted to win. I'd wanted to win so much, I was willing to cheat.

"I'm sorry," I said again, because that was all too terrible to say out loud.

Josh nodded. "Did you really want to be Daniel's girlfriend?" he said.

"*Want* to?" I cried. "No! Of course not! I don't want to be anyone's girlfriend. Ever. In my life!"

Josh nodded again, only this time his cheeks were turning pink, which was annoying because it made my cheeks feel all pink too. "Thanks," he said.

"Thanks?" I said. "Thanks for getting you into this mess? Thanks for embarrassing you in front of the whole school? Thanks for nearly making you cheat because I wanted you to win too much?"

"Thanks for being my friend," Josh said.

Our moms stopped talking about how hard being a parent was. "It's time to go, Josh!" his mom called.

Josh smiled, his cheeks still pink. "I'll see you tomorrow," he said.

My stomach sank — kerplunk — down to my feet. It practically leaked onto the parking lot. We hadn't figured out what to do about the baseball field. I could already hear the shouting and the fighting and the smirking when we saw the fifth graders again. "What are we going to do at recess?" I said.

Josh shook his head. "I don't know. But I'm sure whatever you figure out will be great."

Chapter 12

I practiced four different speeches the rest of that day, and as I fell asleep, and while I ate my sugarless cereal the next morning.

"Relax, Sylvie, everything will be fine," my mom said.

"Your speech sounds good, honey," my dad said.

"When you talk with your mouth full, you look like a fat squirrel," Tate said.

Later, when the bell rang for recess, I walked straight down to the baseball field. One by one, the kids on my team began to follow me. By the time I made it to the field, the whole team was trailing me in a messy line. I was like the Pied Piper of baseball.

I looked for Daniel. I'd promised to stand by him

at recess, and I was not going to break that promise even if I didn't have to be his girlfriend. But Daniel was nowhere to be seen, and the fifth graders were already on the baseball field, only this time they had bats and balls and mitts.

I looked over my shoulder at the kids on our side. They'd brought bats and balls and mitts too. To my surprise, they looked as ferocious as lions. They did not want to get hit in the face with a soccer ball or told they couldn't play hide-and-go-seek. They wanted to play baseball, and they wouldn't settle for less.

We stopped on the edge of the field.

"We beat you," munion number two said. "Josh cheated. The field is ours."

"He didn't cheat," Miranda said. "The spelling bee ended in a tie — Mr. Root said. You both won, so we'll have to take turns."

The fifth graders began shouting that they would never take turns. Our team shouted the same. It was like trying to mix a rabbit with a lizard. There had to be another way. In Tate and Cale's kindergarten class, things had worked out perfectly: Mr. Takaru had decided to get a rabbit *and* a lizard. The kindergarten would have two class pets and everyone would be happy. But it wasn't that easy here. There weren't two fields.

Mr. Root was standing at the top of the playground, watching us. He had his jolly face on, but his fists were on his hips, clenched like a gorilla's. Daniel Fink had appeared. He was standing in his old spot in the trees, watching, listening. He was alone, of course, because he was always alone.

There was a time when I'd thought Miranda didn't want to be my friend anymore. That had been awful. There was a time when Alistair thought he had no friends, back when we started playing hockey. That had been awful for him. I thought about what it might feel like to have two normal legs, then to get cancer, and suddenly you walked funny and people called you Robot Boy. That would make you feel more alone than anything.

"We have to play all together," I said out loud, though no one was listening.

The shouting didn't stop, so I took two steps away from my friends toward the pitcher's mound. "We have to play all together!" I shouted.

Silence fell over the baseball field. I took a deep breath and began my speech. "Everyone wants to play every day, right?"

"Right!" they shouted.

I crossed my arms so my voice wouldn't shake. "There's only one way that can happen! We'll have to play together every day, so no one will be left out."

"No way!" the munions shouted. But they were the only ones. Everyone else shifted their feet. They looked at their elbows. They were wondering if it could possibly work.

Josh stepped up beside me. "Sylvie's right," he said. "The teams will be big if we play together, but we can put extra people in the outfield. Alistair can make sure everyone gets equal turns at bat."

Alistair gave me a high five that wasn't very high because he isn't very tall. "I'm in," he said. "Like a rock."

I had no idea what he was talking about so I gave him another high five.

Jamie Redmond stepped forward. The field went silent again. If Jamie agreed, everything would be okay. If she didn't, we were toast. "Sylvie's right," she said after surveying the crowd. "There's only one field, and I want to play baseball every day. We'll have to play together."

"Awesome!" I said. "We can pick new teams every week."

"And I can make a rotating flow chart so everyone gets to play with each other," Alistair said.

"Rotating flow charts," Jamie said as if she had never heard of those before. "I like it."

Alistair put up his hand to give her a high five and Jamie, in a rare moment of niceness, high-fived him back.

"Who's with us?" I shouted to the crowd.

"I am!" someone on my side yelled.

"Okay!" someone else on my side shouted.

"Let's do it!" called a fifth grader.

"Oh yeah, baby!" shouted another.

"Totally!" said a third, and, one by one, everyone called out their support except for three people:

the munions and Daniel Fink. Daniel was still off in the trees, watching. I smiled at him, but he didn't smile back.

An idea flapped up to my brain and perched there. "Jamie, you pick for Team Cherry," I said, "and Daniel can pick for Team Hill."

"Daniel?" the munions screeched at the exact same time. "You mean Robot Leg? You mean your boyfriend?"

Another hush fell over the crowd, and this time, it was a big one. My cheeks were turning pink again. Oh, how I wanted to punish those munions. I wanted to say something mean that would shut them up forever, but I was so tired of meanness, nothing mean would come. And, suddenly, I didn't want to be mean at all.

Daniel stepped out of the trees. "Sylvie's not my girlfriend," he said.

"We're *friends*," I said before the munions could say anything else.

"And he's my friend too," Josh said.

"And mine!" Miranda called.

"And mine," said so many people, Daniel looked as if he'd been smacked in the face with friends.

Jamie rolled her eyes at everyone. "Come on, Fink. If you're going to pick, you have to stand on the field."

Daniel Fink limped out of the trees and came to stand beside Georgie. "Do you like baseball?" Georgie asked him.

There was silence as everyone on the field listened.

"I love baseball," Daniel said, which is always the correct answer.

Georgie nodded as if he wasn't the least bit surprised. "Then you'd better pick first," he said.

Daniel picked munion number one, but she did not go stand beside him like she was supposed to. She looked at munion number two, who looked as if someone had just stolen all of her mean words, which meant she had no words left. Together, they looked at their old teammates, who took a step away from them as if this was their problem. The munions looked at Jamie Redmond.

"Go stand by your captain," Jamie said, with the biggest eye roll of her life. "You're wasting our time."

Munion number one, with no smirk on her face, slunk over to Daniel. Daniel looked at me and smiled long enough for me to know that everything was okay. He didn't need me to be his girlfriend anymore.

"Scruggs!" Jamie shouted. "You're on Team Cherry!"

"Josh for Team Hill," Daniel called.

I glanced at Josh and caught him looking at me with his small smile. "Since we'll be changing teams every week, I guess it doesn't matter who wins," I said.

Josh nodded at the crowd of kids, some who were good at baseball, some who weren't. Some who had lots of friends, some who had hardly any. They were roaming around, talking to each other like there'd never been a spelling bee scuffle in the first place. "I think this is a different kind of winning," he said.

"And it's just as good," I said.

ABOUT THE AUTHOR

Lindsay Eyre is a mother of five, a graduate of the MFA in Creative Writing program at the Vermont College of Fine Arts, and a fanatical lover of books. She nearly had a heart attack when she had to watch her daughter compete in a school spelling bee, so it's probably a good thing she never made it to one herself. Please visit her website at www.lindsayeyre.com and follow her at @lindsayeyre.

ABOUT THE ILLUSTRATOR

Sydney Hanson grew up in Minnesota with numerous pets and brothers. She is the illustrator of *D Is for Duck Calls*, by Kay Robertson, as well as *The Mean Girl Meltdown* by Lindsay Eyre. She now lives in Los Angeles. Please visit her website at sydwiki.tumblr.com.

Check out all the SYLVIE SCRUGGS adventures!

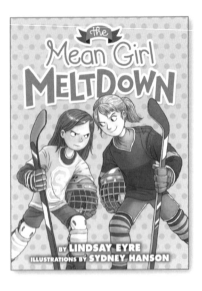

This book was edited by Cheryl Klein and designed by Carol Ly. The production was supervised by Elizabeth Krych. The text was set in Bembo, with display type set in Futura. The book was printed and bound by CG Book Printers in North Mankato, Minnesota. The manufacturing was supervised by Angelique Browne.